# A Magical Birthday Cake For You

Jeannie Dapra, Author

Vicki Newton, Illustrator

Founded in 1957, the SARAH agencies serve more than 1,500 individuals with intellectual and/or other disabilities annually. Our programs and services include residential housing and support, day programs and recreational activities, transitional and employment services, respite care and birth-to-three early intervention services. SARAH's primary goal is to help individuals live fulfilling, productive and engaged lives within the community.

Proceeds from sales of this book benefit the SARAH agencies.
www.sarahfoundation.org

Published by Seacoast Press, an imprint of MindStir Media, LLC
45 Lafayette Rd | Suite 181| North Hampton, NH 03862 | USA

1.800.767.0531 | www.mindstirmedia.com

Printed in the United States of America
ISBN-13: 978-1-7355880-8-7

# Dedication

For every person who has given their heart to a pet and understands the magic of a wagging tail.

For my grandchildren-----Matthew, Natalie, Perrin and Porter who bring love and magical thinking to my life

For Jason, Tippet and Trout who inspired a fun story.

For Richard----Je t'aime

Jeannie Dapra

For Matt and Alex with all my love.

Vicki Newton

SEACOAST PRESS

Once upon a time, there was a brown and white dog named
Tippet. He had a brother named Trout.
Tippet was very smart and well-behaved.
Trout was smart, too, but he was not always well-behaved.
*I know you're smart, but do you misbehave sometimes? We all do!*

There was something different about Tippet, different from all the other dogs—he could bake cakes!
**Really! Isn't that something?**

Tippet loved to make birthday cakes so much he even dreamed about making birthday cakes!

Trout dreamed about eating birthday cakes!

Whenever Tippet wanted to make a birthday cake, he knew, of course, he would get in trouble with his people family, particularly, if they saw him trying to get a wooden spoon from the counter or looking in a cabinet for a mixing bowl. So, as much as he loved baking, he had to keep his secret with only Trout and his friends.

Tippet and Trout loved to talk with their best friend, Jake, who lived next door. Tippet and Trout had many friends—other dogs in the neighborhood, a cat, a robin, an owl, and even a ladybug.

Tippet, Trout and their animal friends had the magical ability to talk with one another!

One day, when some of their dog friends were visiting, Luci, a very big dog, suggested Tippet could bake his cakes when his family was at work, school, or summer camp.

Maxine and Rowdy thought it was an awesome idea. They would help and invite all their animal friends.

So, on   May 10th
when Tippet and Trout's adult family went to work and the
children were off to camp and to school, the baking began!

Jake came by at 9:10 a.m. to help set up the work area.
Tippet measured all the ingredients to make the cakes.

Trout wanted to be helpful, but he kept spilling things and making a mess. Jake knew Trout wanted to be part of the good time, so he spoke nicely to Trout, to help him not make a mess. *You know how that feels, right, to be part of a group that is having fun? Sometimes when Trout was being corrected by his people family, he would close his eyes and cover them with his paws. He thought no one could see him. Isn't that funny?*

By noon, Tippet had made three cakes. Trout put on the icing and sprinkles.
The cakes looked beautiful!

The friends began to join Tippet, Trout, and Jake—Luci, Winston, Ginger the Cat, Rowdy and her sister, Maxine, Sissy, Elvis, Daisy and Casey all gathered in Tippet's backyard under the big oak tree.

Soon, Rosie the Robin, Owen the Owl, and even Annie the Ladybug arrived at the party. They talked, giggled, and laughed. It was a magical time they shared together.

Annie the Ladybug said, "I wish we could sing the Happy Birthday song, but who would we sing it to?"

Trout said, "I know! Let's sing Happy Birthday to "SOMEONE" because every day is someone's birthday."

In their best voices, they sang to all the animals, children, and grown-ups who had a birthday on _____ _____ (*insert child's birthday*).

Maxine said, "I am having such a good time. Is it because we're eating cake?"

"No," answered Tippet. "It's because we all feel the same, even though each of us is different. And, we're being so nice to one another."

What a sweet, charming, happy, magical, and delicious afternoon the friends enjoyed together!

**Don't you wish you could be there too, with all the animal friends?**

At the end of the afternoon, the friends all worked together to
clean up the kitchen and the backyard.
Trout helped by eating all the crumbs they had dropped!

Rosie the Robin flew around and picked-up all the brightly colored sprinkles on the grass.

Trout, Tippet, Jake, Lucy, Owen, Rosie, Winston, Rowdy, Maxine, Ginger, Annie, Sissy, Elvis, Daisy and Casey all agreed Nolan 's birthday was an awesome day!

*You know, many things are magical when you are nice to one another, are happy, and share!*

Jake said to Tippet, "Guess it's time to go back to barking, meowing, and chirping."

Tippet agreed and said, "I really do love our friends! Good friends are such a magical gift!"

And Trout said, "Oh, yes, and I love the cake too!"

When the family came home to a very clean kitchen, they kept saying, "It smells like cake!"

Tippet looked at Trout and smiled a doggy smile, and they both wagged their tails!

The End . . . of this story
And the beginning of many more HAPPY BIRTHDAYS!

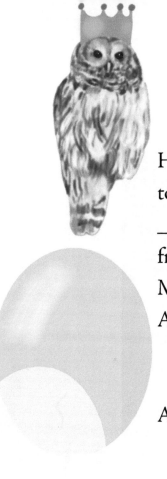

Happy Birthday and very special wishes
to you,

_____NOLAN_____

from Tippet, Trout, Jake, Luci, Rowdy,
Maxine, Winston, Ginger, Owen, Rosie,
Annie, Sissy, Elvis, Daisy, Casey—and
Vicki and Jeannie!

AND _NANA & POP_ WITH LOVE!
      (*book giver*)   MAY 10, 2021

CPSIA information can be obtained
at www.ICGtesting.com
Printed in the USA
LVHW071930261020
669815LV00013B/146